Starry, Starry Night

Starry, Starry Night

Wade Cooper

SCHOLASTIC INC.
New York Toronto London Auckland Sydney
Mexico City New Delhi Hong Kong Buenos Aires

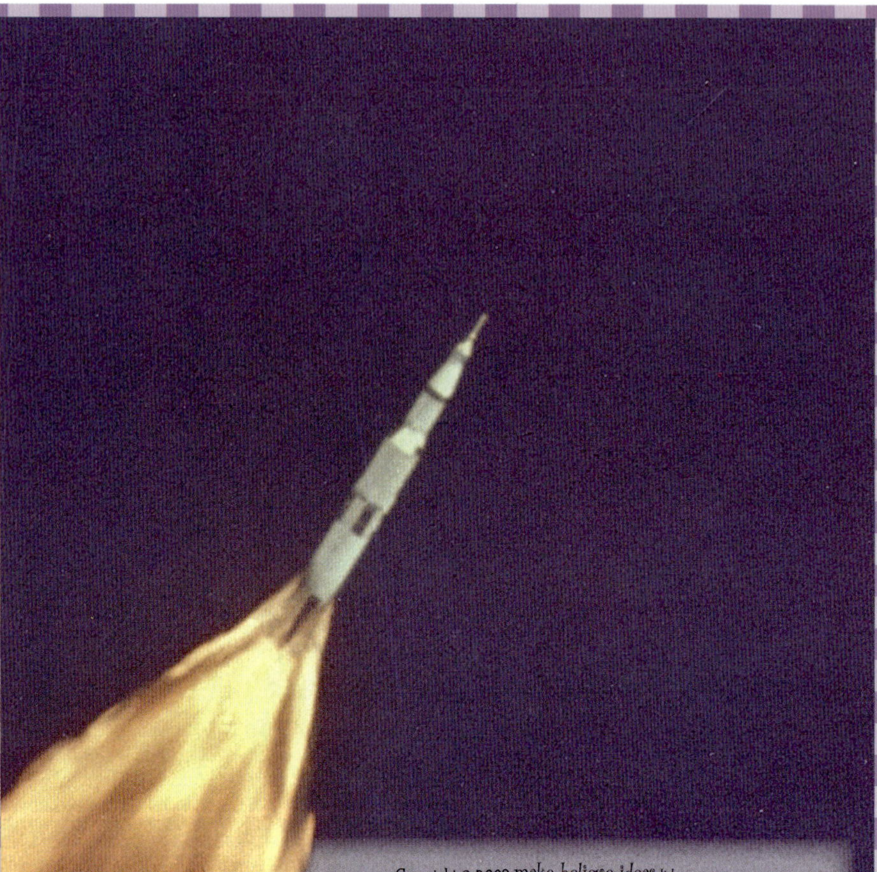

 Published by Scholastic Book Clubs Ltd.

Picture credits
ESA/NASA/SOHO 10, 31br; NASA/HQ 3, 20-21, 29tr; NASA International Space Station Imagery 23mr, 32; NASA/John Hopkins University Applied Physics Laboratory/Carnegie Institution of Washington 14t, 15l; NASA/JPL 1, 14m, 17tr, 17mr, 26-27, 27b, 28mr, 28br, 29ml, 31ml; NASA/JPLCaltech 9, 31tr; NASA/JPL-Caltech/Harvard-Smithsonian CfA 30ml; NASA/JPL/Caltech/Steve Golden 30tr; NASA/JPL-Caltech/University of Arizona 15br, 16b, 31mr; NASA/JPL/Cornell University 5, 24-25; NASA/JPL/GSFC 28tl; NASA/JPL/Space Science Institute 16m; NASA/JPL/STScI 17m; NASA/JPL/USGS 28bl, 31bl; NASA/JSC 3, 18, 30br; NASA/KSC 4, 19; NASA/MSFC 22-23
(t=top, b=bottom, m=middle, l=left, r=right)

ISBN-13: 978-1-84610-987-4
ISBN-10: 1-84610-987-6
10 9 8 7 6 5 4 3 2 1   9 10 11 12 13
Printed in China
This edition first printing, January 2009

Reading together

This book is an ideal early reader for your child, combining simple words and sentences with stunning colour photography. Here are some of the many ways you can help your child take those first steps in reading. Encourage your child to:

- Look at and explore the detail in the pictures.
- Sound out the letters in each word.
- Read and repeat each short sentence.

Look at the pictures
Make the most of each page by talking about the pictures and spotting key words. Here are some questions you can use to discuss each page as you go along:

- Why do you like this picture?
- What does it show?
- What do you think it would be like to be there?

Sound out the words
Encourage your child to sound out the letters in any words he or she does not know. Look at the common "key" words listed at the back of the book and see which of them your child can find on each page.

Test understanding
It is one thing to understand the meaning of individual words, but you need to check that your child understands the facts in the text.

- Play "spot the obvious mistake". Read the text as your child looks at the words with you, but make an obvious mistake to see if he or she has understood. Ask your child to correct you and provide the right word.
- After reading the facts, shut the book and make up questions to ask your child.
- Ask your child whether a fact is true or false.
- Provide your child with three answers to a question and ask him or her to pick the correct one.

Quiz pages
At the end of the book there is a simple quiz. Ask the questions and see if your child can remember the right answers from the text. If not, encourage him or her to look up the answers.

Into Space

What is in space?
People want to know.
Men and women
make machines
that take pictures
of things in space.

This is a picture of a galaxy.
There are many, many
of them in space.
This is a special galaxy.
It is called the Milky Way.
Many, many stars are
in the Milky Way.
Our sun is one
of them.

Did you know?

The Milky Way has
about 400 billion stars.
Our sun is one of them.

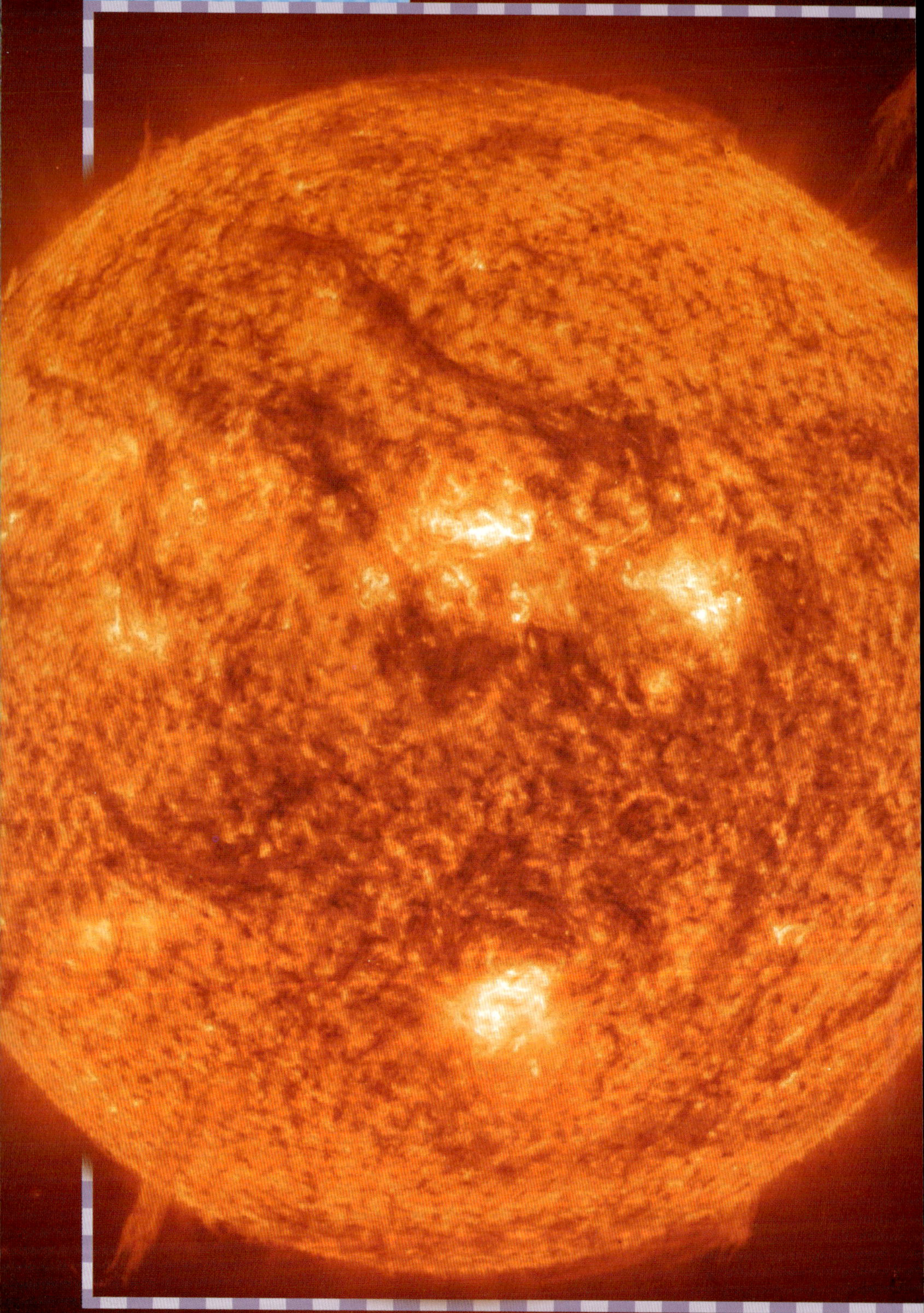

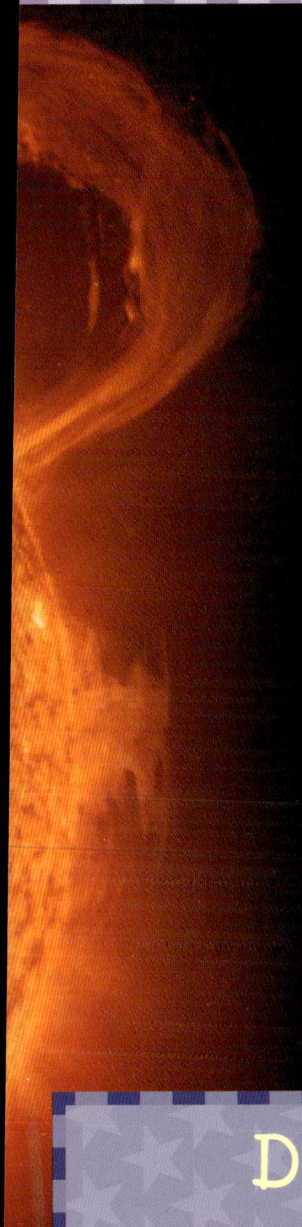

The sun is one star
in the Milky Way.
It is a ball
of burning gas.
It gives us heat
and energy
on Earth.

Did you know?

The sun is very large. You could fit more than one million Earths inside it!

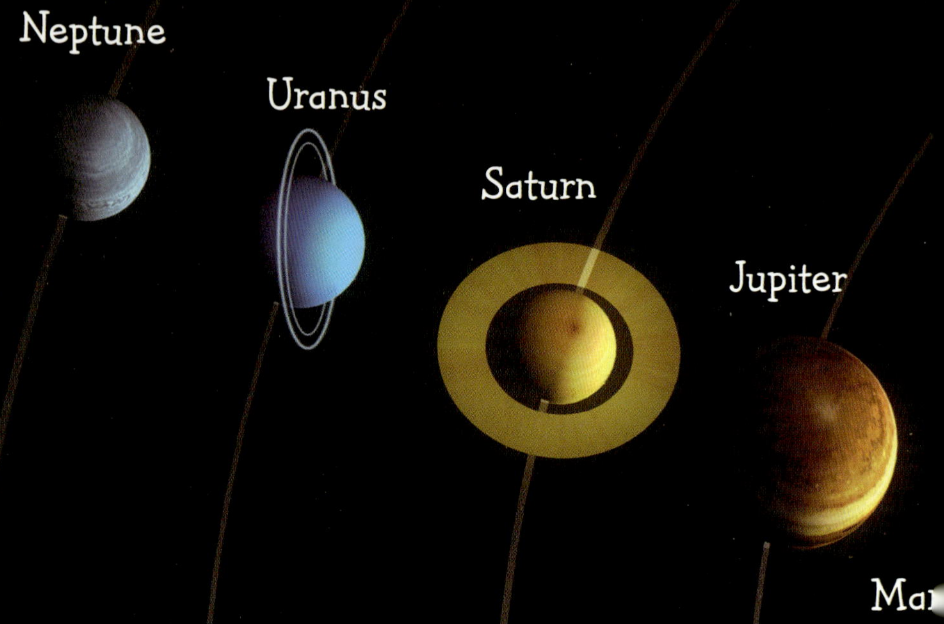

Eight planets go
around the sun.
They are Mercury,
Venus, Earth, Mars,
Jupiter, Saturn,
Uranus, and Neptune.

Did you know?

Asteroids go around the sun, too.
Asteroids are lumps of rock.

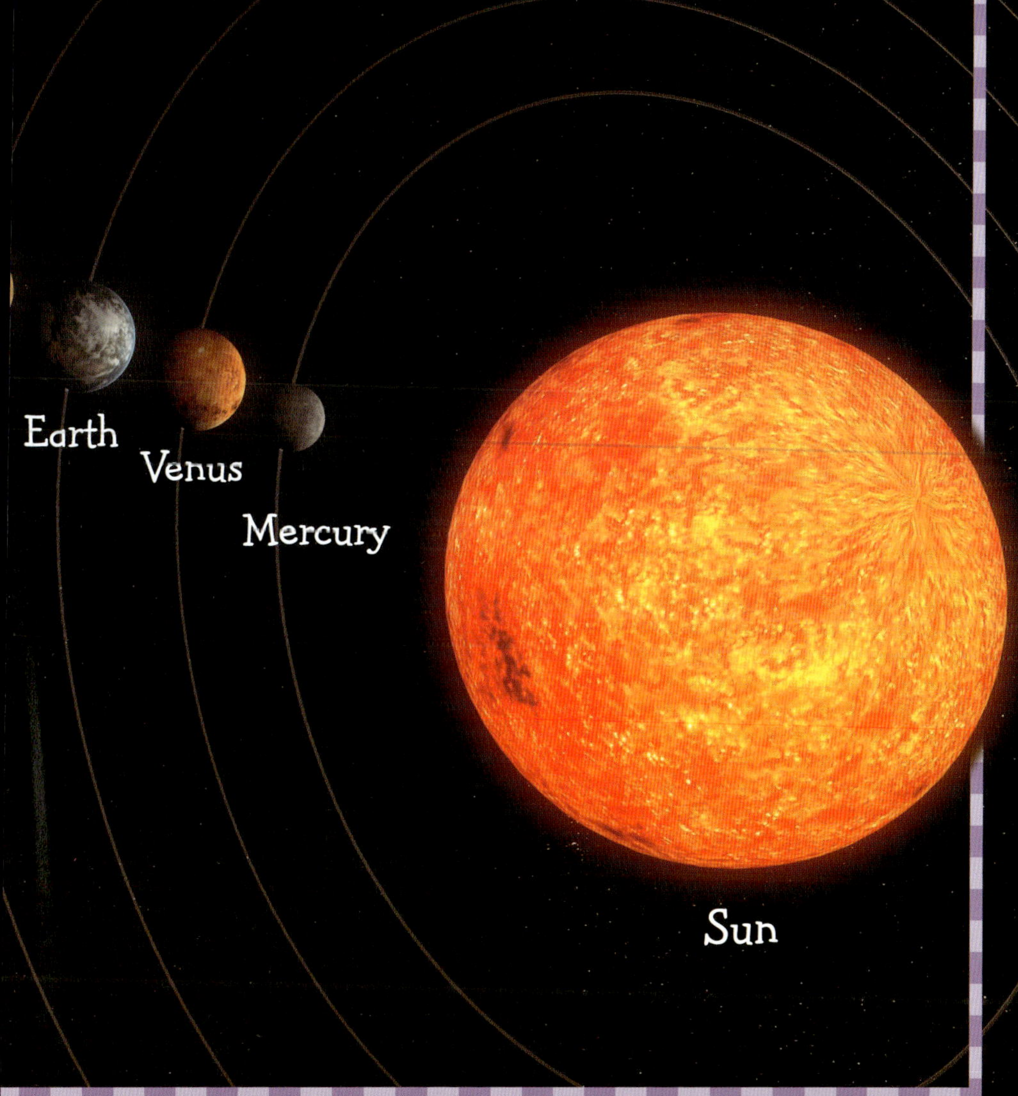

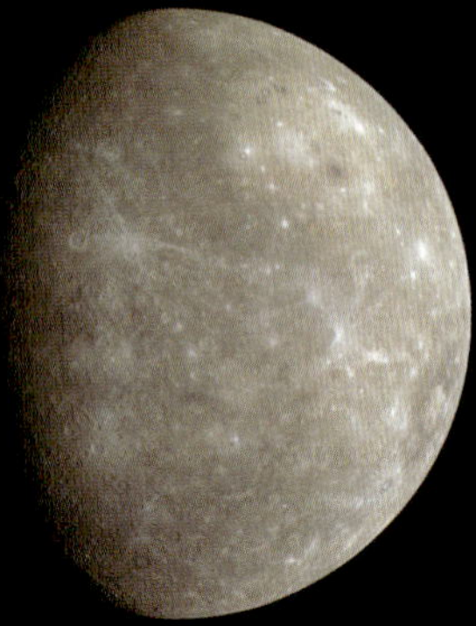

Mercury

Venus

Did you know?

Earth takes 365 days to go around the sun one time.

Mercury, Venus,
Earth, and Mars
are closest to the sun.
They are the hottest planets.
They are made of rock.

Jupiter, Saturn, Uranus,
and Neptune are far
from the sun.
They are very cold.
They are made of gas
and liquid.
They are called
"gas giants."

Uranus

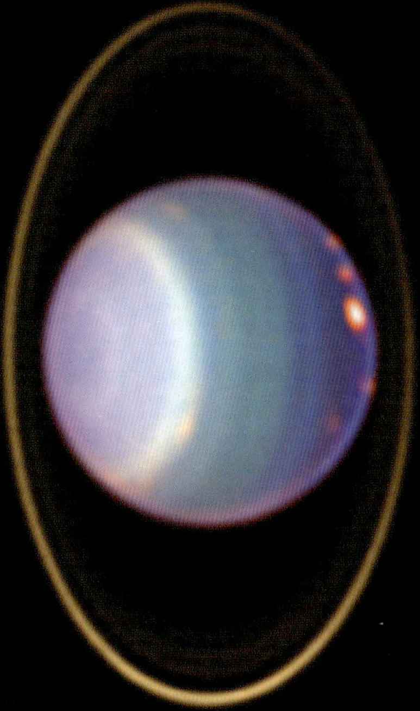

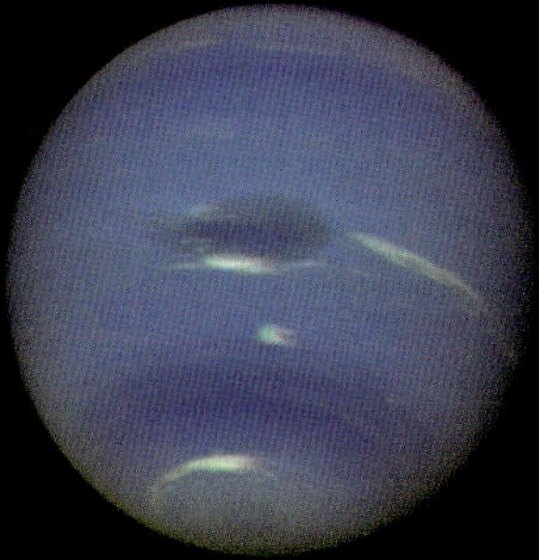

Neptune

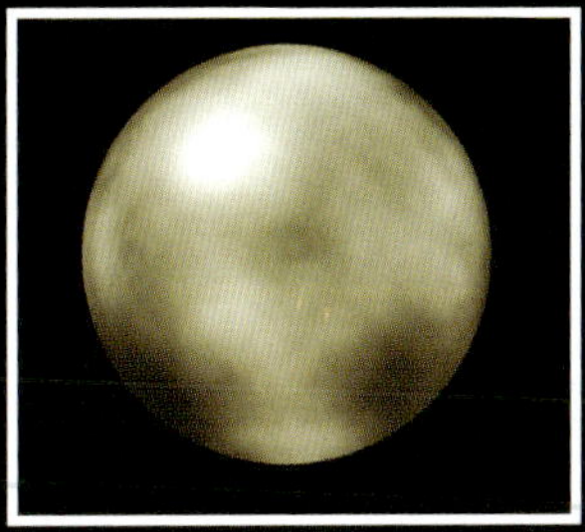

Pluto

Did you know?

People used to call Pluto a planet. In 2006, people stopped calling it a planet.

The first people to walk on the moon were Neil Armstrong and Edwin "Buzz" Aldrin. Michael Collins stayed in the Command Module.

Did you know?

The little white cone holds the crew. It is the only part that will come back to Earth. It is called the Command Module.

Armstrong and Aldrin put an American flag on the moon.

Did you know?

There is no air on the moon. Astronauts carry tanks of air on their backs.

A space station is up in space. Scientists do experiments there.

Did you know?

The space station goes around Earth almost 16 times a day.

People have many questions about Mars.

Did you know?

Mars is rocky and cold. There may be water on Mars.

What does it look like?
Is there life on Mars?
People sent a robot to Mars.
The robot takes pictures
and sends them back
to Earth.

Deep Space 1 went
into space in 1998.
It sent back pictures
of a comet
and an asteroid.
Scientists stopped using
Deep Space 1
in December 2001.
But it is still
out in space.
It will not come back
to Earth.

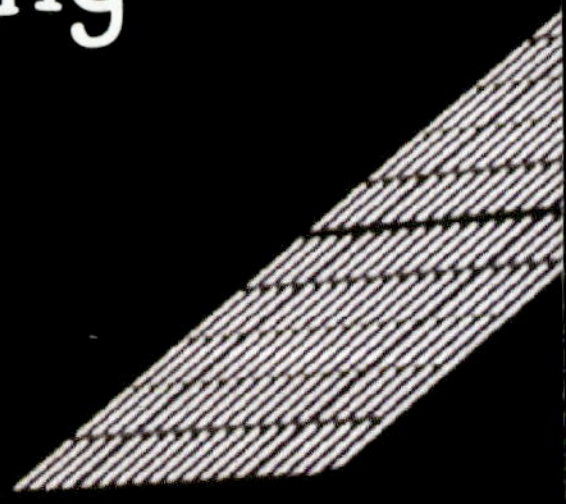

What do you know?

1. What is the Milky Way?

2. How many Earths would fit inside the sun?

3. How many planets go around the sun?

4. How long does it take Earth to orbit the sun?

5. Which four planets are closest to the sun?

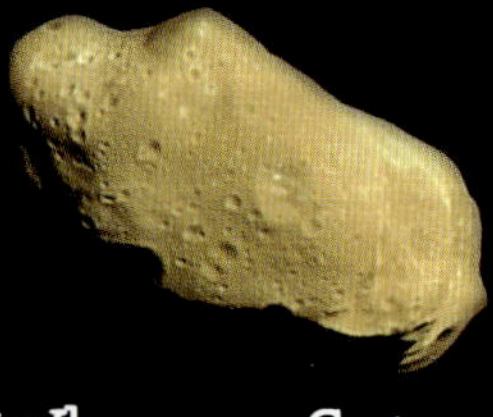

6. What is an asteroid?

7. Why are Saturn, Jupiter, Uranus, and Neptune so cold?

8. Who were the first people to walk on the moon?

9. Why do astronauts need to carry air to breathe on the moon?

10. What is the sun?

11. What is Mars like?

12. What did *Deep Space 1* do?

Answers

1. The Milky Way is a galaxy. **2.** More than one million Earths would fit inside the sun. **3.** Eight planets go around the sun. **4.** Earth takes 365 days to orbit the sun. **5.** Mercury, Venus, Earth, and Mars are the four planets closest to the sun. **6.** Asteroids are lumps of rock that orbit the sun. **7.** They are cold because they are so far from the sun. **8.** Neil Armstrong and Edwin "Buzz" Aldrin were the first people to walk on the moon. **9.** They need to carry air to breathe because there is no air on the moon. **10.** The sun is a ball of burning gas. **11.** It is rocky and cold. **12.** It sent back pictures of a comet and an asteroid.

Dictionary

stars

Stars are large and hot.
They make heat and light.

galaxy

A galaxy is a group of stars.

planet

A planet travels around the sun.

moon

A moon travels around a planet.

astronaut

An astronaut is a person who travels in space.

I • up • look • we • like • and • on • at • for

Key words

Here are some key words used in context. Help your child to use other words from the border in simple sentences.

There **are** many stars in the Milky Way.

Deep Space 1 sent back pictures **of** a comet.

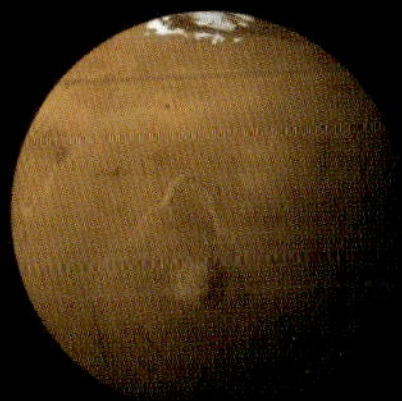

Mars is rocky **and** cold.

There is **no** air on the moon.

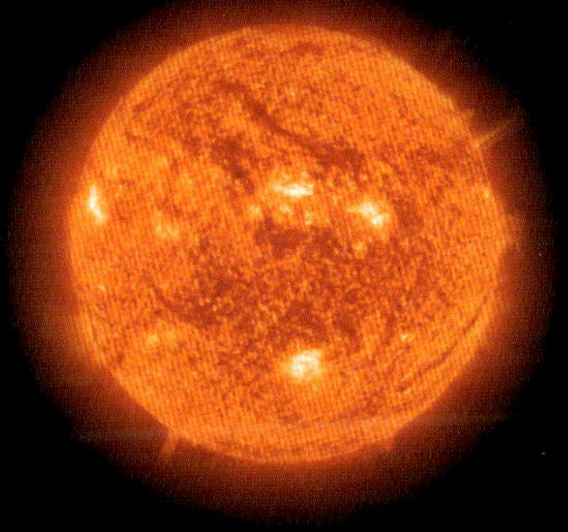

The sun is **a** ball of burning gas.

he • went • many • you • are • this • going • they • play • all • big

the • had • come • my • go • no • is • were

day • get • away • in • of • me • she • see • it • yes • can • am • a